Lonely Pluto

CHARACTERS

Pluto
the smallest and furthest planet from the sun

Venus
second planet from the sun

Mercury
closest planet to the sun

Earth
third planet from the sun

Mars
fourth planet from the sun

Neptune
eighth planet from the sun; Pluto's closest neighbor

Uranus
seventh planet from the sun

Jupiter
fifth and largest planet in the solar system

Saturn
sixth planet from the sun

Sun
father figure to the planets

SETTING

The solar system

Pluto: Ah, me.

Venus: Hey, Mercury, did you hear something?

Mercury: Yes. It sounds like it is coming from the far side of the solar system.

Pluto: What's the use?

Venus: There it is again.

Mars: I heard it, too. It's coming from way out by Neptune.

Neptune: It's not me. It's Pluto. He's sad.

Pluto: Boo, hoo, hoo.

Uranus: There he goes again. He cries all day. He cries all night.

Jupiter: Poor little planet.

Saturn: Let's cheer him up.

Uranus: Yeah. If he stops all that crying, maybe I'll be able to get some sleep.

Jupiter: What's wrong, Pluto?

Pluto: Haven't you heard?

Mercury: Heard what?

Pluto: Some scientists on Earth think that I may not be a planet after all. They say I may be a comet. Or an asteroid. Or even a moon of Neptune!

Neptune: Another moon? I already have eight!

Earth: I have heard scientists that live on me, planet Earth, say that about Pluto, too.

Mars: Those scientists are not always right.

Venus: Pluto is as much a planet as any of us!

Pluto: That's easy for you to say. I'm cold, small, not special at all. But each of you is special in some way. Mercury, you are closest to the sun.

Mercury: All nine of us planets love the sun. So I am lucky to be so close.

Pluto: You get to be hot, hot, hot—over 800 degrees. I'm always cold, cold, cold because I am the furthest planet from the sun! I am so far away that the sun has probably forgotten me.

Venus: I'm sure that's not true.

Pluto: Venus, you are the second planet from the sun. And you are so bright in the sky. People on Earth can see you without a telescope. They call you the Evening Star.

Venus: Darling, I like to be seen. But that's not everything.

Earth: Well, Pluto, at least you have privacy.

Pluto: Earth, you are the third planet from the sun. You have it best. You have life on you! Life! People, plants, animals.

Earth: I really can't complain. I am happy. Except when people don't take care of me.

Pluto: And Mars, you are so cool-looking. You are red. Plus, people on Earth study you.

Mars: That's because some scientists think that I may have had life on me a long time ago.

Pluto: Then comes Jupiter, the biggest planet. Mighty Jupiter! King Jupiter! Look at tiny me! Why, I'm even smaller than Earth's moon!

Jupiter: Since you brought up moons, I have so many that I lost count. And I am so big, more than 1,000 Earths could fit inside me.

Saturn: Jupiter may be biggest, but I am the most beautiful.

Venus: Um … Saturn, you're not helping matters.

Pluto: No, it's okay. Saturn has a right to be proud. Look at those beautiful rings.

Saturn: But you have inner beauty, baby.

Uranus: Saturn is not the only planet that has rings. So do I, Uranus.

Saturn: Yes, but I have more rings. And they are easier to see. My rings are made of dust and ice.

Uranus: My rings are made of black spinning chunks. Some Earth scientists say the chunks look like lumps of coal.

Pluto: Spinning black chunks! That's cool.

Neptune: Speaking of cool, do you know that I have the strongest winds of any planet? They can blow more than 1,000 miles per hour.

Uranus: Wow! That does make you special, Neptune.

Pluto: Then there's me. Cold, small, not special at all.

Jupiter: Gee, the little planet really is feeling bad.

Mars: There's only one thing we can do.

Earth: Are you thinking what I'm thinking?

Mars: It's time to ask the big guy for help.

Venus: The sun? Yes, of course! He'll know what to do.

Jupiter: Are you sure we should bother him? He's always so busy.

Saturn: One of his planets is upset. Trust me. He'll want to be bothered.

Mercury: I'll ask him. After all, we're very close. Oh, Sun!

Sun: Yes, Mercury?

Mercury: We need your help. It's Pluto. He is feeling left out and not special at all.

Sun: You bring me sad news, Mercury. I'll talk to Pluto. Oh, Pluto! Pluto!

Pluto: Who's that? Who's calling lonely Pluto?

Sun: It is me. The sun.

Pluto: Sun! You haven't forgotten me!

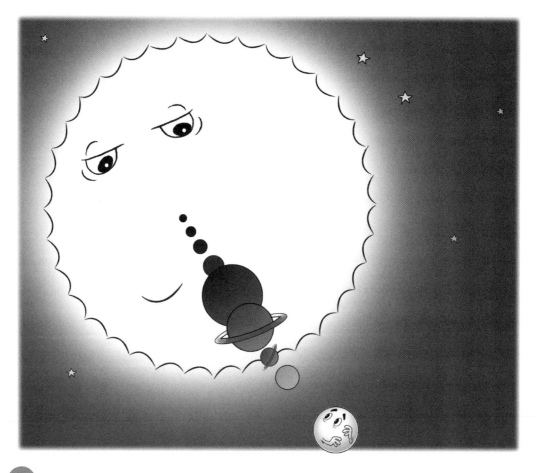

Sun: Forgotten you? How could I? You are one of my nine planets.

Pluto: But I'm billions of miles away from you. I'm cold, small, not special at all.

Sun: That's not true. You're just as special as any of the other planets. I can prove it.

Pluto: How?

Sun: First, you have the longest orbit around me. One year on you would last 248 years on Earth. Even more important is that the children on Earth love learning about me and my solar system. But they have trouble learning the names of my nine planets. And they have trouble remembering their order in my solar system.

Pluto: Like me being last.

Sun: That's why Earth children have a special saying to help them remember the names of the planets and their order. Do you want to hear it?

Pluto: Sure.

Sun: My Very Eager Mother Just Served Us Nine Pizzas.

Pluto: I don't get it.

Sun: The first letter of each of those words is the same as the first letter of the name of each of the planets. Mercury, Venus, Earth, Mars, Jupiter, Saturn, Uranus, Neptune, Pluto. You try saying it.

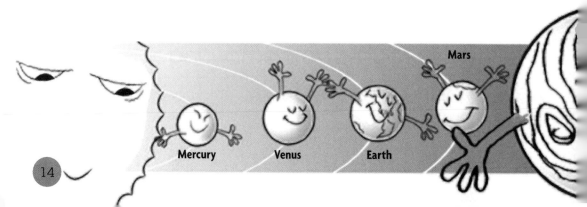

Pluto: My Very Eager Mother Just Served Us Nine Pizzas. Hey, I'm "Pizzas"!

Venus: You sure are, darling!

Sun: You're the best part of that sentence!

Pluto: "P" for Pluto and "p" for pizzas.

Earth: Most children I know love pizza. It's one of their favorite foods.

Pluto: I love pizza, too!

Mercury, Venus, Earth, Mars, Jupiter, Saturn, Uranus, and **Neptune:** We all love pizza!

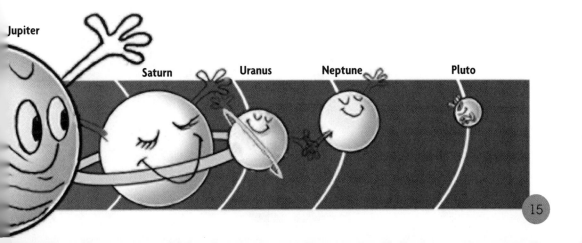

Sun: So, you see, Pluto, the children need you. My solar system needs you!

Pluto: Wow! Thanks, Sun. Thanks, everyone. I may be cold and small, but I *am* special after all!

Sun: Now, who wants to have a pizza party?

Mercury, Venus, Earth, Mars, Jupiter, Saturn, Uranus, Neptune, and **Pluto:** We do!

The End